Dear Parents:

Congratulations! Your child is taking the first steps on an exciting journey. The destination? Independent reading!

STEP INTO READING® will help your child get there. The program offers five steps to reading success. Each step includes fun stories and colorful art or photographs. In addition to original fiction and books with favorite characters, there are Step into Reading Non-Fiction Readers, Phonics Readers and Boxed Sets, Sticker Readers, and Comic Readers—a complete literacy program with something to interest every child.

Learning to Read, Step by Step!

Ready to Read   Preschool–Kindergarten
• big type and easy words • rhyme and rhythm • picture clues
For children who know the alphabet and are eager to begin reading.

Reading with Help   Preschool–Grade 1
• basic vocabulary • short sentences • simple stories
For children who recognize familiar words and sound out new words with help.

Reading on Your Own   Grades 1–3
• engaging characters • easy-to-follow plots • popular topics
For children who are ready to read on their own.

Reading Paragraphs   Grades 2–3
• challenging vocabulary • short paragraphs • exciting stories
For newly independent readers who read simple sentences with confidence.

Ready for Chapters   Grades 2–4
• chapters • longer paragraphs • full-color art
For children who want to take the plunge into chapter books but still like colorful pictures.

STEP INTO READING® is designed to give every child a successful reading experience. The grade levels are only guides; children will progress through the steps at their own speed, developing confidence in their reading.

Remember, a lifetime love of reading starts with a single step!

Copyright © 2025 Disney Enterprises, Inc. and Pixar. All rights reserved. Published in the United States by Random House Children's Books, a division of Penguin Random House LLC, 1745 Broadway, New York, NY 10019, and in Canada by Penguin Random House Canada Limited, Toronto, in conjunction with Disney Enterprises, Inc.

Step Into Reading, Random House, and the Random House colophon are registered trademarks of Penguin Random House LLC.

Visit us on the Web!
StepIntoReading.com
rhcbooks.com

ISBN 978-0-7364-4426-2 (trade) — ISBN 978-0-7364-9044-3 (lib. bdg.)
ISBN 978-0-7364-4427-9 (ebook)

Printed in the United States of America

10 9 8 7 6 5 4 3 2 1

Random House Children's Books supports the First Amendment and celebrates the right to read.

STEP 2 READING WITH HELP

STEP INTO READING®

Disney · PIXAR

Elio Goes to Space!

adapted by Cynthea Liu
illustrated by the Disney Storybook Art Team

Random House 🏠 New York

Elio is unique—
he is one of a kind!
His greatest wish
is to go to space.

Elio spends most of his time alone. He wonders if he is *too* unique.

Elio lives with his aunt Olga.
She works for the military.

One night, Olga gets a strange message. What does it mean?

Aliens have finally arrived for Elio! A beam of light pulls him into a spaceship.

Elio cannot believe what he is seeing. Space is amazing! He never wants to leave.

The aliens make a new cape and boots for Elio. He is ready to explore!

Ooooo is a supercomputer.
Her job is to help Elio.

Ooooo makes a copy of Elio.

This copy goes to Earth to take Elio's place.

Elio speaks to
all the aliens.
They think he is
the leader of Earth.

Later, Elio meets Glordon.

He wraps Elio in a web.

Elio is scared at first.

But Glordon is just a kid! They are not so different from each other.

Elio and Glordon become friends.

The aliens find out Elio is not the leader of Earth. They send him home. Olga is happy to have the *real* Elio back.

Then a spaceship crashes nearby. It is Glordon! He needs help.

Elio and Olga work together to save him. They help him get back to space.

The aliens are proud of Elio for saving Glordon. They ask him to stay.

Elio loves space, but his home is on Earth with Olga.

Now Elio will always know that he is not alone in the universe.